TRUST DADDY

PEPPER NORTH

Pepper North
With a Wink Publishing, LLC

AUTHOR'S NOTE:

The following story is completely fictional. The characters are all over the age of 18 and as adults choose to live their lives in an age play environment.

This is a series of books that can be read in any order. You may, however, choose to read them sequentially to enjoy the characters best. Subsequent books will feature characters that appear in previous novels as well as new faces.

AN INVITATION TO BE PART OF PEPPER'S LITTLES LEAGUE!

Want to read more stories featuring Zoey and all the Littles? Join Pepper North's newsletter. Every other issue will include a short story as well as other fun features! She promises not to overwhelm your mailbox and you can unsubscribe at any time.

As a special bonus, Pepper will send you a free collection of three short stories to get you started on all the Littles' fun activities!

Here's the link:

http://BookHip.com/FJBPQV

CHAPTER 1

"Sorry, lady. The estimator did a terrible job quoting you an amount for the move. It's going to be an extra three hundred dollars for us to get the last of your things out of the van." The burly man looked at her with a vaguely threatening expression.

Samantha pictured the inside of her new duplex. Jumbles of boxes were piled here and there, regardless of the labels she'd marked on them. The company she had hired based on recommendations from friends had been a nightmare from the beginning. Now they wanted more money? "We have a contract," Samantha began, trying to make her voice sounded firm.

"Like I said, lady, the estimator did a bad job."

"Maybe I should just call your boss," she suggested, pulling her phone out of her back pocket.

"The office closed a half hour ago. He's gone for the weekend. We can just take the stuff and dump it off at head-quarters. You can come to pick it up when you want," he suggested as he moved to the side to show her that all that remained in the van were the most massive pieces of furniture.

Even if she had a truck to move them, she'd never be able to lift those items by herself. She stared at the man in disbelief. Were there any good men out there?

"Any problems here?" a deep voice sounded behind her. Samantha whirled around to see a police officer in full tactical gear standing on the lawn behind her.

Overwhelmed, words tumbled from her mouth, telling him way too much. "My husband of twenty-two years had an affair with a floozy at the gym. I lost the house in the divorce settlement, causing me to have to move here. Now, this man is holding my furniture hostage until I pay him an extra three hundred dollars. How's that for problems?" To her horror, tears burst from her eyes as the pity party she'd been holding off for weeks crashed over her.

The officer walked forward and wrapped an arm around her waist. Automatically she turned toward him, accepting any shred of human compassion. "Please show me in the contract where it says that you may change the rate at the last minute," the police officer requested.

"Oh, don't fall for her drama. You know how it is with women. She's trying to cheat us out of our pay."

"What?" Samantha's tears evaporated as she got angry. "Look, asshole…" she sputtered.

The muscular arm around her waist tightened, and Samantha closed her mouth with a snap. "The contract, please."

This time it was the moving man's turn to speak hesitantly. "You know, they usually give us one of those… They must've forgotten to put it in the truck this time."

"Then, you really don't know what's in the contract. I can track down the owner and have him brought to the station with his copy," the police officer assured the man.

"Oh! That won't be necessary. I tell you what, we'll just get the last of this furniture out of the van. I'll be sure to report the estimator on Monday." He signaled the other two men who had been standing in the shadow of the nearby tree.

As three of them jumped into the back of the van, one assistant asked, "Did you get the extra money?"

"Shut up!" the man hissed as they quickly got back to work.

"How can I ever thank you?" Samantha wiped the tears from her cheeks. She knew she was a hot, sweaty mess and now had streaks of mascara everywhere. She looked at the police officer's name tag. The shiny metal plate announced Cpl. Adams. A strip of black on silver drew her attention. His badge was wrapped in a black ribbon. Samantha knew what that meant.

Instantly, she felt ashamed of her petty problems. "I'm so sorry. This has been an awful day for you. Go home and take care of yourself." She stepped back, away from his body.

"I'm going to stand right here and make sure they place all of your belongings safely in your house. I'm your neighbor, Blake Adams. I'm glad I was here to help."

"I don't usually cry all over my neighbors," she tried to explain. Her mind raced back over all the information she blurted out. She felt the heat build in her cheeks and knew she was blushing furiously.

"Then, let's be friends instead of neighbors. I'm going to grill steaks outside tonight and drink a few beers in honor of my friend. I'd love to have some company," he suggested.

Knowing that the young officer in his thirties couldn't be attracted to a plump woman in her forties with two-inch gray roots, Samantha smiled and accepted. It wouldn't matter what she looked like. "I'd love to join you. I don't have any food in the house, to be honest. No, that's a lie. I have cookies that I can contribute for dessert."

The men carried the remainder of the furniture in quickly. To Samantha's delight, the crew actually listened to her and placed the final items where she wanted them.

Corporal Adams remained outside on his quiet vigil. He quickly became her favorite man on earth.

She studied him surreptitiously. The man was carved from muscle, his face partially concealed by polarized sunglasses. Samantha decided that he wasn't attractive. His features were too coarsely chiseled for that. He was, however, as masculine as hell. In fact, she could see him as the main character in the romance novels that she loved so much. He was the perfect Daddy.

When the back gate on the moving van rumbled down into place, Samantha felt as if someone had lifted a weight from her shoulders. Turning, she thanked him once again. "Corporal Adams, I hope that there's ever anything I can do for you, you'll ask. Thank you so much for your help today. That could've gotten really ugly."

"I'll talk to his boss on Monday. Extortion is against the law. I'm intrigued to know if it's just that crew or if the entire company is corrupt." The officer held up his hand to stop her from protesting his investigation. "I know. It's not anything I have to do. It's something I want to do." A devastating grin spread across his face, transforming it. "I like the good guys to win as many times as possible."

Joining in his laughter, Samantha tried not to stare. How could she ever have judged him as unattractive? "I must need glasses." When one of his eyebrows quirked upward, she realized she'd said that out loud. To cover up her revealing statement, Samantha blurted, "You have to be the best neighbor a girl could ever have!"

"I can't stand to see someone take advantage of a Little girl." Before she could react to his words, the officer turned and walked to the front door next to hers. "You can call me Blake, for now, Samantha. I'll meet you in the backyard in one hour. Dress comfortably. And oh, bring those cookies if you can find them."

Samantha tried not to stare as he turned to enter his side

of the duplex. The view was absolutely as good going as it was coming. Hurrying into her own door to shower and try to find the cookies, she realized that she was smiling for the first time in six months. Her friends tried to tell her that her rat of a husband had done her a favor by cheating. With her heart breaking, Samantha had never thought she'd enjoy anything again. One more thing to attribute to Corporal Adams—no, Blake.

CHAPTER 2

B lowing out a nervous breath, Samantha hesitated in the doorway. Did he really want her to join him? She didn't want to impose on her new neighbor. He'd already helped her out so much.

"Come on out. I'm getting ready to put the steaks on," Blake's deep voice commanded. He turned slightly to wave an encouraging hand.

She followed his directions without a second thought. Emerging on the concrete patio that stretched along the back of the duplex, Samantha lifted a nervous hand to wave hello, then dropped it to tug at the hem of her shorts. They were comfortable but way too short for someone of her weight to wear. Emotional eating had always been her weakness.

"Sit in the pink chair, would you?" he asked as he ignited the coals in his grill.

Taking several steps forward, Samantha spotted the two chairs sitting on the concrete slab. One was high-backed and a beautiful pastel pink. The other was a navy blue, boring lawn chair. She eagerly sat down on the fabric seat. Her short legs barely reached the ground when she scooted her bottom back in the chair. Kicking her feet, Samantha allowed her eyes to roam over the hard body in front of her.

He had to be in better shape than any man she'd known. Way better shape than Darrell, she thought cattily. Her ex-husband had been the star of their high school team, while she'd been a cheerleader back then. Darrell had loved her plush figure, a bit curvy even in her teens. But as time went by, he had been unhappy with the few pounds she gained each year.

She guessed that Blake was in his early thirties. His thick black hair had begun to thin slightly at the back. Somehow that minor flaw made him even sexier. Her fingers itched with the desire to brush through the closely cropped style. She guessed he cut his hair for convenience rather than to adhere to the most popular fad.

When he looked back to see her staring at him, Samantha felt she needed to say something, "How long have you worked for the police department?"

"I enrolled in the police academy when I finished my degree in criminal justice. I've been with the department for nine years. What do you do?"

"I'm a graphic artist. Or, as my ex-husband describes me, I sit around all day and color." Samantha's tone was dismissive and self-ridiculing. She'd heard Darrell complain about her job almost since they first got married.

"Stop that." Blake's voice was commanding.

Swallowing hard, Samantha blinked as she looked at him in disbelief. He wasn't upset with her because she talked badly about herself, was he? "Sorry," she said automatically to appease him.

"Stop that, too."

She sat there silently for several minutes, watching him tend the grill. Samantha started to wiggle forward to get her feet on the ground. Perhaps it was better if she went inside.

Freezing at his next words, Samantha looked at him incredulously.

"I won't allow you to talk badly about yourself. I don't know what bullshit that ex-husband of yours drilled in your head, but here, it's not allowed." He turned and stalked back to sit in a lawn chair close to her. "He's gone. His loss."

"I'm not sure how much he..." Samantha stopped talking when Blake lifted one warning eyebrow. She noticed that his eyes were green—a beautiful emerald green. The artist inside her craved paper and color pencils. His face was magnetic and compelling.

"Here, you need to rehydrate." Blake handed her a bottle of pink lemonade. When she twisted the bottle to see how many calories it held, he removed it from her hand and opened the cap for her. "Shrug off those things you've worried about in the past. Just enjoy being settled and free."

Automatically, Samantha lifted the bottle to her lips. It tasted so good. "Thank you," she said simply. "It's delicious."

Blake stood up. Samantha expected him to go check on the grill. To her surprise, he moved in front of her to place his hands on her chair's armrests. He was so close. Samantha took a deep breath and held it. Blake smelled slightly of smoke from the grill, cloaking a spicy, masculine scent underneath.

"This is the last time I will say anything about your jerk ex-husband. He was a fool to let you get away. I won't be that unwise." Blake lifted one hand to cup the back of her head as he leaned forward. His lips captured hers. Heat burst between them as he demanded entry into her mouth. Obediently, she opened her lips to allow his tongue to sweep inside. The taste of delicious male made her toes wiggle in delight.

How long had it been since anyone had treated her as desirable? Samantha clung to the armrests, wanting to touch him but afraid to interrupt this moment. She did not want this to end. When his lips lifted from hers, she leaned forward, automatically chasing the pleasure he had bestowed.

He paused inches away from her face. Those green eyes seemed to memorize her face. The hand behind her head prevented her from shrinking back in embarrassment. "Little girl, you're the best thing I found." Blake's gentle tug on her ponytail sent an electric shock to her core.

When he stood back up, Samantha tried not to breathe heavily in reaction to their close encounter. Her mind tried to rationalize the kiss, and her defenses kicked in to protect her. "Why are you doing this? I've been through enough. I don't need you to make fun of me, too?"

His eyes hardened. "I'm going to ignore that tone, Little girl. I know that idiot hurt you, and you'll need proof that I'm not like him. Will you let me prove that to you?"

Unable to draw her gaze from his, Samantha found herself nodding. A sense of rightness settled inside her. "Yes," she whispered. His answering smile made her heartbeat jump irregularly. *Damn, he's hot.*

"Drink your lemonade," he directed.

When he turned around to place the grate on the grill, Samantha collapsed against the chair's back. Obediently, she lifted the bottle to her lips and took a sip. Licking her lips, she savored the remnants of Blake's kiss and found herself wishing for him to kiss her again.

Hearing her mind away from that thought, Samantha blurted the first question that came to mind, "Why do you keep calling me Little girl?"

He glanced at her before placing the steaks on the grate. The sizzle and smell of the grilling meat made Samantha's stomach growl in hunger. Blake smiled at the loud sound as he came back to sit next to her. Extending a hand toward her, he squeezed her fingers in approval when she placed her hand on his. "I have a feeling you know exactly what a Little girl is. The Daddy inside me has searched for the one meant for me. I know I found her now. Does that scare you?"

Here in the duplex's backyard, Samantha paused as she listened to the sounds of the neighbors and kids playing outside on a beautiful evening. Her world had narrowed to the small bubble of space that wrapped around Blake and herself. It felt safe and protected, as if she could be honest. "It should, but it doesn't," she whispered.

"Good girl," he praised. "You've had an interminable day. I suspect you had some pretty tough weeks before that. Let's just get to know each other tonight. Tomorrow we can have a serious conversation. Just know, I'm not going to let you run away. I've searched too long for you."

Samantha nodded. She didn't know what exactly was happening, but she felt it, too. An undeniable bond between them had clicked into place. Suddenly, the future looked so much better. Leaning back in the beautiful chair, she swung her feet in silent celebration as he dealt with their dinner.

An hour later, she pushed the plate to the edge of her lap. Her stomach was happier than it had been for a long time. She'd been eating crap for weeks. Rocked by the divorce decree that mandated the house she'd lived in for over twenty years be sold, Samantha had packed nonstop for days. She'd rented a dumpster for all the photos, mementos, and other reminders of their lives together. Darrell had walked away from everything. Precious things suddenly had no value.

The sadness that had overwhelmed her had dissipated. For the first time, getting rid of all that junk felt good. "Thank you for dinner," she told the fascinating man.

"I've enjoyed your company. Got any room for dessert?"

"Oh, I forgot the cookies!" Samantha wiggled to the edge of her chair to stand.

"Hold on to those cookies. You'll need the energy to unpack those boxes. I have something else you might like.

Give me just a minute." Blake picked up her plate and his to disappear inside his home. In just a few minutes, he returned with two long, yellow, frozen tubes.

"I haven't had one of those Popsicles for years," Samantha enthused.

"They make this kind for big Little girls," Blake explained, stripping off the top with scissors, the cold tube with a napkin wrapped around it to hold.

"Mmm! This has alcohol in it!" Samantha licked her lips. The frozen ice tasted just like a fancy lemon drop drink. She savored it quickly, enjoying the flavor before it melted.

"Not too fast, Sami," he warned.

"I haven't been called Sami for a very long time. Darrell didn't think it sounded sophisticated enough."

Blake raised his frozen treat to her in celebration. "Idiot."

Squirming in her chair, giggles burst from her lips. She had a few more bites of the delicious treat. "I really like these."

"They're dangerous. Eat it slowly." Blake shook his head at her but smiled. "Your giggles are infectious, Little girl. I'm going to make sure I hear more of those. I have a feeling you haven't laughed in a while."

Samantha tipped up the plastic tube to drain the last of the delicious treat into her mouth. She shook her head. "Nope. Idiot."

His laugh filled the air, deep and filled with clear enjoyment. Samantha loved it. Holding the empty container out to him, she asked, "If it's not incredibly rude, can I have another?"

"I think your moving in calls for a celebration. Let me grab another round."

CHAPTER 3

S amantha rubbed her face against the scratchy blanket. She was so warm. Despite the rough surface under her cheek, she'd slept better than she had for a long time. Knowing that boxes were waiting to be unpacked, Samantha forced her eyes open and froze.

A broad masculine chest filled her view. Samantha lifted her right hand to brush across one massive bicep to check if she was hallucinating. Her questing fingers touched hard, warm flesh. Moving her head slowly, her gaze trailed the thick muscles of his neck up to that chiseled face. Blake.

His arms tightened around her slightly to hold her in place. "Little girl, you feel good in my arms." His voice was low and growly, sending shivers of awareness to her core. She'd thought his voice was sexy last night.

Now, she could feel her body reacting to the pure masculinity that wrapped around her. His thigh pressed between her thighs against the pink polka-dotted panties she'd put on after her shower. He couldn't feel her getting wet, could he?

Samantha tried to shift away from his pelvis and froze once again. He was hard. Thick and hot, his erection pressed against her soft tummy. She sucked in her belly, trying to disguise the extra pounds she knew she needed to lose.

A warm hand pressed against her back, pinning her to his hard frame. "Don't try to be anything but you. I love your beautiful curves."

"Blake, I don't know how I got here, and I am way too old for you." Samantha pushed against his muscular chest.

"Whoa, Little girl!" His arms tightened around Samantha, holding her in place. "I want you to listen to me for sixty seconds. At the end of that time, if you still want to flee, I promise I'll let you."

Samantha nodded. What could he say in one minute that would convince her to stay?

"That second ice pop did you in. You curled up in your chair and napped. When I woke you, you admitted that you had nowhere to sleep. I brought you in here and tucked you in bed. And you being too old for me is garbage. If it doesn't bother me, should it bother you?"

Shocked, Samantha forgot that she'd been struggling to get away. "It's not that easy."

"It is. I am attracted to you, and I believe the feeling is mutual. Does it really matter if you've been on this earth longer than me?" That eyebrow quirked up again over one beautiful green eye. Mesmerized, she slowly shook her head. Blake leaned in to kiss her.

His mouth moved slowly over hers. Teasing and tasting, his lips beguiled her. When she lifted her chin to deepen the kiss, Samantha earned a reward. His tongue dipped into her mouth. A low groan of arousal echoed into the quiet room. That sexy, low voice had an immediate effect on her libido.

Wiggling closer to him, Samantha tried to eliminate the small gaps between his hard body and her soft flesh. He felt so good! Without conscious thought, she rubbed her full breasts against his chest. One of his hands cupped her ample bottom. She froze in self-consciousness for several seconds before Blake pulled her flush against his thick erection.

That was not the reaction of the man who was turned off by her figure. Throwing caution to the wind, Samantha decided to ignore her doubts. She would enjoy his body and his attention while she had the opportunity. Others lived for the moment. Why shouldn't she?

That hand caressing her bottom slid under the edge of the T-shirt she wore. As he eased it up her body, Samantha allowed herself to explore Blake. Her fingers glided over his chest and shoulders, tracing the grooves of muscles. She'd never been with a man in this incredible form. She protested being interrupted from her discoveries when he pulled the garment over her head.

"Shh, Little girl. You can play again soon."

When she emerged, Sami daringly traced her fingers down the scattered hairline on his abdomen. When she touched the silken flesh on the head of his penis, Blake ripped his mouth away from hers to growl a warning. "Little girl, you're playing with fire. It's time to stop me now if you don't want this to go any further." His eyes blazed with desire.

Rubbing herself against the hard thigh between her legs, Samantha whispered, "Please!" She clung to him as Blake rolled Samantha quickly onto her back. His mouth took hers in a blazing kiss that took her breath away.

When he lifted his head to stare down at her with desire etched on his face, Blake claimed her. "Mine!" Holding her gaze until Samantha nodded in agreement, Blake rewarded her with another devastating kiss before beginning to taste her skin as he pressed his lips to the sensitive column of her neck.

Samantha clung to him. Reflexively, she dug her nails into his shoulders when he lightly bit the skin at the curve of her shoulders. His groan of desire matched hers. Blake captured her hands and pinned them to the pillow under her head. Automatically Samantha struggled to pull loose. The thrill of being overpowered pushed her desire into a level she'd never felt before.

"Settle down, Little girl. Daddy's in charge," Blake ordered in a gruff tone.

"Daddy?"

"You will call me Daddy, Little girl. When you're ready…" His voice trailed off as Blake returned to kissing her body. His lips closed over one taut nipple.

Engulfed in the heat of his mouth, Samantha felt his tongue swirled around the puckered tip. With a quick breath in, she lifted her chest toward him, seeking more. Blake rewarded her by drawing firmly on the tightened bud. She protested wordlessly with whimpered sounds when he abandoned one breast but calmed as his lips closed over her other needy peak. His hand cupped her full mound to raise it to his mouth.

Releasing her with a pop sound, Blake complimented, "So beautiful!"

For once, Samantha didn't question his words. His expression and hard shaft pressed against her revealed his genuine desire. She basked in the appreciation in his gaze. It had been so long since she'd seen the lust in her ex-husband's eyes. She realized the favor Darrell had done for her in ending their marriage. She felt a seductive smile curl the edges of her lips. Urging Blake on silently, Samantha lifted her pelvis to press tightly against his erection.

Blake shook his head. "No, Little girl. There's no way I'm rushing this." He slid down toward the bottom of the bed, kissing the fiery path down the center of her body. Hovering over those pink polka-dotted panties, he inhaled. "So sweet," Blake murmured against the thin fabric.

His teeth closed over the thin fabric, raking her mound slightly. When she shivered underneath him, Blake pressed her hands deep into the soft pillow. "Keep your hands here, Sami," he ordered. When she nodded, he pushed the covers over the bed's end to reveal her body completely. Surprised, she automatically cooperated as he drew the last scrap of fabric from her body.

Blake moved to the end of the bed and easily slid her body down to the edge. As he knelt, he pressed her thighs apart and settled between them. When seconds passed and he didn't touch her, Samantha moved her arms to prop herself up onto her elbows. Blake stared at the flesh he'd revealed, her skin free of hair. Blake glided his fingertips over her denuded mound.

"Oh, Little girl. You are more beautiful than I could have imagined." Her small sound of surprise drew his attention. "Don't be naughty. I would enjoy spanking your full bottom. Back into position," he ordered.

Immediately, she flopped back down to the mattress. Abandoning any attempt at being graceful, Samantha only wished to follow his directions. She strained to watch, cursing her full breasts, which impeded her view as his head lowered to the junction of her thighs. She felt the warmth first of his skin and then the searing heat of his tongue as he lapped through her pink folds. The rumble of his "mmm" as he tasted her vibrated through her most sensitive area. Clenching her fingers into the pillow, Samantha forced herself to stay in position.

His mouth devoured her. Nibbling and sucking, Blake explored her intimately. When one thick finger glided into her narrow channel, Samantha tried to lift her pelvis closer to his lips. He quickly controlled her movements with one firm hand on her hip. Samantha knew Blake was in charge. She would have to take all that he lavished on her body. Closing her eyes, she savored the sensations building within her.

Two fingers replaced the one to stretch her. It had been

so long since anyone had touched her intimately. Sami moaned at the burning pleasure. His lips closed around that bundle of nerves at the top of her channel to distract her. Sucking lightly at the bud, Blake continued to prepare her.

Her juices flooded from her as her arousal grew higher than anything she had felt before. Samantha pushed her old regrets from her mind. *Concentrate on this!* She was rewarded as his teeth closed gently over her clitoris. A fast, intense orgasm flashed over her body, leaving her panting at its impact. A keening sound echoed from deep inside her. His caresses gentled to prolong her pleasure.

Blake glided his fingers from her vagina to trail lower to that small, hidden entrance between her buttocks. When she gasped and tried to close her legs, his body blocked her automatic movement. Circling that tight entrance, Blake claimed possession of her body. "There is no part of you that will be off-limits. Wherever I wish to touch, your body will open to me." His finger coated with her slick juices pressed inside.

No one had ever touched her there. Forbidden desire lanced through her body, raising her pulse once again. *He wouldn't want to take me there? Would he?* Samantha bit her lower lip as she tried to stifle her sounds of arousal. Surely this shouldn't turn her on?

"Let me hear you, Little girl. Don't hide anything from your Daddy," he commanded. When she nodded and allowed her lips to part, Blake added, "Daddy knows your secrets." When she wailed in reaction, Blake's low chuckle rolled over her body as his finger invaded her fully. Samantha sighed in relief when that thick digit slid slowly from her body.

His hands spanned the top of her thighs, holding them wide apart. Blake rose smoothly to his feet. "Stay just like this, Little girl. I want to protect you." When she nodded without understanding the message behind his words, Blake walked along the side of the bed, trailing his fingers over her body. Dropping a hard kiss on her lips, he opened the nightstand drawer to withdraw a small packet.

Samantha's eyes fixed on the powerful hands as he tore the packet open. Unable to look away from his thick erection, Samantha watched him roll the condom over his shaft. A thread of doubt wove through her mind. *Will he fit?*

As if sensing her nervousness, Blake's hand stroked over his penis. "Don't worry, Little girl. Daddy will always take care of you. Will you trust me?"

"Yes," she whispered. His smile lit a glow inside her. She wanted to make them proud of her.

His body stalked to the end of the bed, and he dropped effortlessly to his knees. Blake pulled her further off the edge of the bed, so her hips balanced precariously. Samantha froze in place as he shifted closer to press the broad head of his erection against her entrance. Slowly, he glided forward, forging the path inside her.

Samantha fought to their hands in place. She begged, "Please! I need to touch you!" When he nodded, Samantha reached forward to touch his broad chest. Her fingers were eager to explore his body once again.

Blake's hands tightened on the top of her thighs. She knew he battled to move slowly and give her time to adjust. Samantha tried to lift her hips, but he held her anchored in place. His warning glance reminded her that Daddy was in charge. She'd never been with a lover who put her needs in front of his. In awe, Samantha tried to memorize this moment.

When his hips met hers, they both groaned at the exquisite sensation. He filled her completely. Samantha couldn't imagine this getting any better, but she wanted him to move. She bucked up slightly against him, trying to urge him on. Blake chuckled and withdrew. Each thrust forward came a bit quicker until she clung to him for support.

Samantha tried to wrap her legs around his waist, but

Blake would have none of that. He simply lifted each thigh to drape her leg over his broad shoulders. He was in control, not her. That twisting grind at the end of each stroke fueled the sizzling heat between her legs. She could feel her orgasm lurking just out of her control. Samantha gyrated underneath him, unable to remain still.

There! Her eyes closed as an explosion of pleasure poured over her body. Her channel clamped desperately around his massive erection, earning a groan of pleasure from his lips. As the sensation faded, she peeked through her lashes. Seeing his face emblazoned with desire thawed a bit of the self-doubt that had been festering inside her. "You make me feel so good," she whispered to the powerful man between her thighs.

"I'm never letting you go, Little girl. Come with me!" he demanded. His thrusts increased, lavishing pleasure on her body. She wrapped her hands around his forearms as he reached forward to caress her body. Anchoring herself on him as the sensations began to buffet her body again, Sami clung to him. With a sudden cry, she felt her body spasmed around him.

A guttural shout burst from his lips as he stilled between her legs. Then with several short grinding thrusts, Blake ensured that her pleasure extended as he joined her. Finally, he slumped over her body, supporting his weight on his forearms. Blake rested his forehead against Samantha's as their raspy breath merged together.

When their heartbeats had slowed, Blake's eyes opened to gaze into hers. "There's no going back now."

CHAPTER 4

Sitting quietly at the breakfast table, Samantha studied Blake's form. She'd tried to run away after their amazing sex, but Blake had simply wrapped his arms around her and held her close. Feeling his heart beat against her, Samantha had relaxed in his embrace. Her desperate urge to potty interrupted their quiet recovery time a few minutes later. Chuckling at her red face as she revealed her need, Blake released her to allow her to scurry to the bathroom.

Upon her return, he dropped her discarded T-shirt over her head before taking her hand. When he led her into the kitchen, she followed him obediently. It just felt right to follow his directions and sit down at the table while he made breakfast.

Allowed only to observe, Sami used her time to study him. Dressed only in a pair of baggy basketball shorts, Blake's body was the sight to behold. Her eyes narrowed at the sight of a scar just below his shoulder blade. She knew he had a dangerous job. That wound underlined the peril.

"Why are you a police officer?" she bluntly asked.

"It's what I am. My dad was a cop and his dad before him. I think it runs in my DNA." Blake turned from the stove, holding a hot skillet. He heaped scrambled eggs on her plate until she held up her hand in protest. He turned to dump the rest on his plate before dropping the skillet in the sink.

She watched in disbelief as Blake sat down at the table and began eating. There was no way that he could eat that much. As if reading her mind, Blake answered her, "I'm a big man, Little girl. It takes a lot to fuel my body. Eat." He motioned to her plate.

Samantha picked up her fork and took a bite of the fluffy eggs. "These are good," she said in surprise. Blake just laughed at her tone. Silence stretched between them before Samantha blurted, "I didn't know Daddies really existed." Then feeling her face heat, she explained, "I mean not a relative daddy, but a Daddy with a capital *D*. I've read a lot of books. I always figured people didn't actually live like that. You know… with cribs and bottles? It's fiction, right?"

"People live in age-play relationships. There are probably more than you realize. We'll find some friends for you to play with, and you'll have a chance to ask the Littles questions when you're ready." Blake reached out to caress her face. He smiled when she turned to press her cheek against his palm.

"I don't think I'm ready for that," she confessed.

"Okay." Blake steered the conversation to more superficial topics.

Samantha found herself telling him everything from her favorite color, pink, to her childhood pet, Stinky. She was pleased to learn more about him, as well. He fascinated her. Open and willing to share, he was the direct opposite of so many people in her life.

When she had eaten all that she thought she should, Samantha pushed the plate away from her. She didn't want to look like a hog. To her surprise, Blake filled his fork with eggs and lifted it to her lips. "Oh, I can't eat anymore."

"Five more bites for Daddy," he directed. Keeping the

conversation flowing smoothly, Blake continued to alternate feeding himself and then her until she had taken those required bites. "Can you eat any more?" he asked softly. "The truth, this time."

Samantha slowly shook her head. "I'm full now."

"Always tell me the truth, Sami. Would you like to know what rules I will require of you?" Blake asked before scooping another large bite of egg into his mouth.

"Rules?" she echoed.

"Little girls need rules to follow. Otherwise, they might make poor choices." Blake finished the eggs in one last bite. Standing to clear the plates out of their way, Blake grabbed a large tablet of paper and pen. At the top of the page, he wrote in big letters, "Sami's Rules."

Samantha stared at those black, block words. A shiver went down her spine. "What happens if I don't follow those rules?"

"I could send a naughty Little girl to stand in the corner or to bed early. If you endanger yourself or our relationship, your punishment will be a spanking or more."

"More?" she repeated.

"Yes. Your punishment will be in line with your offense." Blake scooted back from the table and patted his lap. "Come sit on my lap, Sami."

"I'm too heavy," she protested.

Blake reached around her to grab the back of her chair. Using that as a handle, he pulled her easily to him. After scooping her out of her chair, he sat her on his lap. Blake wrapped his arms around her to hold her in place when she would have scrambled away. "You are not too heavy. I will hold you in my arms often." He steadily held her gaze until she nodded. "Good girl. Rule number one, follow Daddy's instructions. Rule number two, do not lie to Daddy. What else do we need to make a rule?"

"Do Daddies love their Little girls?" Sami whispered with her heart in her throat.

"Rule number three, Daddy and Sami will care for each other completely."

Staring at the letters on the page, Samantha realized that he had committed them to a relationship that she'd never really had. Tears poured from her eyes. She never cried after Darrell had asked her for divorce, refusing to let him see that she was upset. Now wrapped in this amazing man's arms, she felt safe.

Blake didn't ask questions. He held her close and rocked her body from side to side. Talking to her quietly, he reassured her about happy he was to find her and how idiotic her ex-husband had been. He also informed her he would never, ever, have an affair. "I'm not looking for a meaningless relationship. I found you, Little girl. I don't plan on ever letting you go. I think we need to change rule number two." He crossed out the first thing on his list. Above it, he wrote, "Daddy and Sami will always be honest with each other."

Wiping the tears from her cheeks with balled-up fists, Samantha whispered, "Thank you."

"Thank you, Sami, for coming into my life." Blake leaned forward and kissed her, not with the passion that had filled his kisses earlier. This kiss held promise and hope in its gentle caress. When he lifted his head, Blake pressed one more kiss to the tip of her nose as if he couldn't get enough of her sweetness. "I have something special to show you. Will you come with me?"

Samantha nodded eagerly. She clutched his shoulders when Blake effortlessly lifted her off his lap to stand by the chair. Backing up so he could move, Samantha accepted his hand when he offered it. With a wide grin, Blake tugged her down the hall to a closed door.

"I put this room together when I first moved in. I was sure that I would find my Little girl quickly and wanted to be ready for her. I never would've guessed that she would have to find me," Blake said before opening the door. He stepped back to let her enter first.

Walking into the sunlit filled room, Samantha's gaze jumped from place to place. Overwhelmed, she had no idea where to focus first. Blake's warm hand on her low back grounded her. She took a deep breath and let it out. Turning to look at him, she asked, "It's a nursery?"

"Yes, Little girl."

She turned to look over his shoulder at the entrance before rotating to look at the entire room. The walls were painted a pale yellow. Here and there, a striped tiger stuffie frolicked and played. She loved him on sight. Orange with black stripes, he had a long tail and whiskers. Pointing out one illustration, Samantha asked, "Who's that?"

"It's very sad. He's played in here for a long time with no one here to give him a name," Blake shared.

"Everyone needs a name!"

"Perhaps you can think of a name for him."

Nodding, Samantha turned her attention to other things in the room. She pointed at a large bed with railings around it. "Is that a crib? It's too big for a baby."

"It's made for an extraordinary baby—an adult Little girl."

She clapped a hand over her mouth. It wasn't that she was totally shocked; she just barely kept herself from asking if it was hers. Blake would find someone much more suited to be his Little. He was very nice and maybe a bit attracted to her, but this wasn't the room for someone temporary.

"Would you like to lie down in the crib?" Blake softly suggested. The hand low on her back urged her forward.

Stiffening her legs, Samantha resisted. It wasn't fair to whoever this room would be suited for as their forever home. "I don't want to take over someone else's bed. I wouldn't like an imposter lying in my place."

Blake stepped in front of her. Tilting her chin up with an

unyielding hand, he looked her squarely in the eyes. "Little girl, remember rule number two? Daddy and Sami will be honest with each other. You are not an imposter."

"Really? You want this to be my room?" Her voice squeaked with incredulity.

"I want this to be my Little girl's room. I'm surer than I've ever been that you are the one I've been searching for and dreaming about for years. Now, let's try this again. Would you like to jump up in the crib?" he asked with a gentle smile.

Her head nodded before Samantha realized what she was doing. Her heart made the leap of faith that her self-protective mind resisted automatically. This time she allowed him to guide her to the railing protecting the crib. She watched him trigger a lever at the base of one corner post.

As the railing lowered, Samantha leaned in to touch the beautiful, buttercup-yellow quilt that covered the mattress. A faint puff of dust rose from the soft fabric. She looked back at Blake. No one had slept in this bed for a very long time.

"Let me take that dusty thing off. I'll throw it in the washer today." Blake carefully folded the quilt to avoid spreading the accumulated dirt on the pristine sheet below. He dropped it out of the way and sneezed when a cloud rose from it. Covering her face to muffle her giggles, Samantha convulsed into full laughter when Blake wrapped his arms around her and pulled her body against his.

"Beware! I am the dust monster!"

"Daddy, don't get me dirty!" she protested, pushing away, and then squeaked as his arms tightened around her once again.

"Say it again!" he urged as he set her away from his body to peer into her eyes.

"What did I say?" Samantha said in confusion. She said something wrong? She replayed her sentence in her mind and realized what he wished her to repeat. "Daddy?"

Blake wrapped his arms around her waist and lifted her

feet from the carpet. Twirling in a tight circle, he laughed. He sounded so happy that Samantha joined in his celebration. When she was utterly dizzy, he lifted her to set her bottom down on the crib's mattress. Blake leaned in to capture her lips in a triumphant kiss. His mouth dominated hers, making her clutch at the sleeves of his T-shirt for stability.

When he raised his head, his expression was joyous "Thank you, Little girl. I'm so glad our paths crossed."

With a blare, the phone in his pocket exploded with noise. Blake pressed one last quick kiss on her lips before standing and answering the phone. "Adams, here." His voice changed instantly into a stark, professional tone. "I will be there in ten minutes. Establish a perimeter."

"I'm sorry, Sami. I have to go. You're welcome to stay here and explore the nursery."

"Go. I'll go back to my apartment and start unpacking boxes." Samantha looked around the room. She would have loved to play here for a while and ignored the work that waited for her next door. As she scooted toward the edge of the mattress to slide off, Blake lifted her easily with a hand on each side of her waist.

"Your keys are on a rack at my back door. I locked up for you after you fell asleep. No running away, Little girl! We made so much progress. Take the list of rules on the kitchen table with you. I want you to unpack your art supplies first and make two signs of the rules—one for your side of the duplex and one for mine. Leave space at the bottom," he commanded.

"For more rules?" She spoke before thinking.

"For whatever we need." Blake turned around and gave her a sharp smack on the bottom that made her jump forward with a yelp. As she glared and rubbed her bottom, he leaned over to pick up the dusty quilt, ignoring her reaction. Pacing forward, Blake swept her into the hallway where he stopped for a moment to kiss her one last time.

Samantha continued into the kitchen where she looked on the rack for her keys. She considered the piece of paper on the table. Debating, she almost decided to leave it where it was, but her bottom still smarted slightly. She snatched up the paper and took it with her. How bad could it be if she lost it in the jumble of boxes?

CHAPTER 5

B lowing her bangs off her forehead, Samantha looked around in triumph. There were still numerous boxes to unpack, but at least she had everything in the right room now. Her bed was made, and she had dishes and her coffeepot in the kitchen. Things were looking up.

She glanced out the large front window for the hundredth time. Blake hadn't returned yet. Looking at the clock she'd just hung on the wall, Samantha tried to keep herself from worrying. He'd been gone for ten hours. How long of a shift did he have to work?

After jumping in the shower, Samantha grabbed her keys and headed out the door. A trip to the grocery store was next on her list. Blake's side of the driveway remained empty. *He's a grown man. He doesn't need his next-door neighbor to worry about him.*

When she returned and unpacked all the groceries, Blake was still away. Exhausted after unpacking all day long, all Samantha wanted to do was go to bed, but she couldn't—without knowing if he was okay. She picked up the key ring with her new apartment key on it. She loved the declaration that hung from the ring. It was a pink sparkly unicorn. This morning she noticed an extra key. She had a hunch about what door it opened.

Letting herself out at the back door, Samantha locked it before walking just a few feet to Blake's. Tentatively, she slid the unknown key into the lock and turned it. *Click.* The handle turned, and she pushed it the door open.

Blake's house was dark and quiet. Samantha turned the dead bolt and hung the sparkly unicorn key ring on the empty rack. Walking to the kitchen, she noticed that everything seemed less vibrant without its owner there—as if someone had sucked out all the energy when he left. Steadying herself with a hand on the wall as she yawned, Samantha's last vestige of energy dissipated.

Without another thought, she turned into the nursery and walked to the crib. Kicking off her shoes, Samantha hopped up to land on her knees on the soft mattress inside. She stretched out and sighed in contentment. The enclosed bed felt as good as she remembered. As her eyelids fluttered shut, Samantha rolled onto her tummy and wiggled until she was comfortable.

* * *

The standoff had been long and drawn-out. Unable to storm the house due to the two small children inside, the police had chosen to negotiate from a distance. Finally, the suspect's mother was located and transported to the scene. Badly shaken by the details the police had pieced together, the new arrival convinced her daughter to send the kids out to her. As their grandmother, she had been there to hug and reassure the frightened children.

From their conversation with their grandma, the police had gained confirmation that an argument between their parents had become violent. The father had threatened his wife with a knife. When he lunged to stab her, the woman had defended herself. Unfortunately for them, the kids had seen their mother kill their father. A social worker on the scene took command of the trio.

Considering this new information, Blake delayed the SWAT team, who were now ready to fill the house with tear gas before going in to capture the woman. He called her cell phone one last time. "Cynthia, the kids told us what happened. We know you're upset. We also know that you acted in self-defense. Before the situation goes any further, please come out so I can help you?"

Silence met his request as she considered his words. Thirty seconds later, she responded, "Are you going to take me to jail? I just want my kids to be safe."

"You acted in self-defense. We know your husband attacked you with the weapon. You're allowed to defend yourself," he reassured her. He'd seen this before, a woman who had suffered for years before finally fighting back. In the violence's aftermath, she'd panicked. Unsure what to do when the police surrounded the house, the woman had hidden inside.

"Can I trust you?" she whispered.

"Your little girls need you just as mine needs me. There'll be an investigation, of course. As long as the evidence matches your accounting of the event, you'll be released from custody quickly."

The front door cracked open. The thin, shaking woman walked through the door holding both hands above her head. Immediately an officer was there to handcuff her and escort her to a squad car. The situation ended. Now, it was time for the investigation to begin.

"Well done," his police lieutenant complimented. Doug Stone leaned in to ask confidentially, "You found your Little girl?"

"I did." Blake accepted the slap on the back and congratulations. A small core of Daddies on the police force had

31

discovered each other. Some were still looking for their perfect Little. The lieutenant was one of the lucky ones. He'd known his Little since they were in second grade. "Think Lettie would be interested in a playdate?"

"My Lettie is a bit shy, but she loves to meet new Littles. We'll coordinate later. For now, head to the station and write up your report. Then, head home to that precious Little girl," the lieutenant ordered.

"On my way."

Two hours later, Blake pulled into his garage. Seeing all the lights on in Samantha's house, he frowned. This late at night, she should be sound asleep. He knocked on her door, but no one answered. Wonder grew inside him. Could his Little have gone to visit him?

He let himself into his side of the duplex and toed off his creaking leather shoes. Walking through the pitch-black rooms, Blake appreciated his ability to see well in the dark. The nursery door was open. As he headed directly to the crib, Blake could see an outline of a figure inside. Each step brought him closer to the view he wished to remember forever. Samantha lay curled on her side with her hands tucked under her cheek.

Pulling his phone from his pocket, Blake couldn't resist taking a picture of this precious sight. Staring into the crib, Blake felt all the stress of his day evaporate. *How has she become so vital so quickly?* He leaned against the railing at the head of the crib. When his equipment belt rattled against the wood, Samantha sleepily murmured, "Daddy?"

He reached in to brush his fingers through her silky brown hair. "I'm here, Sami. I'm glad you came to sleep in your crib."

Her eyes blinked open to meet his. "I couldn't resist," she admitted.

"I'm glad. Would you like to stay here in your crib to sleep, or would you rather join Daddy in his big bed?"

"Daddy's bed."

Blake leaned into the crib and scooped his Little girl into his arms. Holding her close, he bent to kiss her lips lightly. "I like that choice." Turning, he carried her from the room, ignoring her sleepy protests that she was too heavy and that she could walk. Samantha would learn that she needn't worry about his strength. She felt perfect in his arms.

Setting her feet on the carpet next to his bed, Blake tossed back the covers before helping her slide into bed. "I'm going to take a shower. Someone would like to keep you company." Holding up one finger to ask her to wait, Blake disappeared into his closet. He quickly stored his weapons in the safe before searching. In a box underneath the hanging clothes, he had stored something precious for his Little.

As he returned, Blake switched on the light in the master bathroom to illuminate the room slightly. He did not want to miss her reaction. With a smile, Blake held the plush tiger out to Samantha. Tentatively, she reached out to the floppy orange-and-black-striped stuffie. Samantha sat up to examine it closer.

"It's the stuffie on the walls! He's so cute! He's the one without a name!" she protested, squeezing the soft creature to her body.

"It's very sad that he doesn't have a name. He's been waiting for me to find my Little forever. Doesn't he look happy now?"

She nodded immediately as small lines of worry appeared between her brows. "The stuffie needs a name."

"Yes. You think of one while I take a shower."

"Me?"

"Little girls come up with the best names. He wanted you to decide. Lie back and think about it," Blake directed. When she complied, he rewarded her with a kiss.

He hesitated at the doorway to the bathroom as he unbuttoned his shirt. Hearing her voice as she talked softly to the tiger, Blake knew between the two of them, they'd come up with the perfect name. He turned to take a quick shower. Blake couldn't wait to hear what she decided.

Ten minutes later, he emerged to find Samantha fast asleep and curled up in bed around the tiger. She'd obviously worked very hard when he'd been away. Moving quietly, Blake slid into bed behind her to spoon his exhausted Little. He inhaled deeply, enjoying the clean scent of the woman he still couldn't believe had found him. Blake wrapped an arm around her waist, pulling her snug against his body. Within minutes, he, too, was asleep.

CHAPTER 6

The sun filled the bedroom by the time Blake woke up the next morning. Samantha was glad to see his beautiful green eyes. She'd been awake for a couple of hours and had thought about getting up but didn't want to disturb him. She enjoyed the opportunity to study his impressive form as the sheet drooped dangerously low over his hips. The man was definitely eye candy.

"Morning," she greeted him. Moving the stuffed tiger between their bodies, Samantha growled a greeting for him as well. "Rwahr!"

"Good morning to both of you. To whom do I have the pleasure of speaking?" Blake asked formally. His voice was low and gravelly with sleep.

"Choosing the name for a stuffie is a serious business. We both liked Cheeto for a little while, but that was too close to cheater, and neither one of us like them. I thought of Regit, but he didn't like that one because you have to spell backward. So, we settled on Grrr!"

"Grrr? I think I like that. It's a perfect name." Blake reached a hand forward to lift one floppy paw. "Nice to finally know your name, Grrr." Blake wrapped his arms around them and pulled the duo close before rolling them over so that he was poised above them. "Excuse us, Grrr. I need morning kisses from my Little girl."

Plucking the stuffed tiger from her hands, Blake laid him on the pillow beside them. He turned to look down at her. "Sami, I was very pleased to find you in your crib last night." He pressed soft, sweet kisses to her lips.

Samantha didn't try to stifle her soft sounds of pleasure as she clung eagerly to his broad shoulders. His pelvis nestled against her. She could feel his eager response to being close. All the doubts that had floated through her head of how he could be attracted to her disappeared. He was. She pushed all the other stuff out of her mind. Blake had decided that she was his. Samantha wasn't going to argue with him.

When he lifted his head, she stared up at his passion-filled expression. She hoped he'd always look at her this way. Something deep inside her clicked into place. Who cared if he was younger than she was?

"There's my Little," he said softly. "I have a day off today. Can we spend it together?"

Thrilled, she agreed, "I'd love that."

When Blake rolled away to stand next to the bed, Samantha tried to figure out what he was doing. The sight of him standing nude wiped most questions from her mind. When he cleared his throat to draw her attention, she realized that she missed noticing the hand he extended to her. Feeling her face heat with embarrassment, Samantha quickly placed her hand in his and allowed him to pull her out of the covers. She was way overdressed.

"We need to get a nighty for you to wear," he observed, taking in her leggings, oversized T-shirt, and socks. "Do you need to potty before we have breakfast?"

"Mmmm, what about...?" She gestured at his raging erection.

"If you're good, Daddy will let you play with his penis later. For now, go potty and meet me in the kitchen," he directed.

"I'm not hungry," she lied. She'd already been awake for a couple of hours, and her stomach had growled repeatedly. She could ignore it for a little while longer.

"Little girl, Daddy decides when you may have pleasure. Now, it's breakfast time. Are you ready to do what I've asked, or should we review rule number one?"

"I don't care about the rules. I'm not planning on following them," she distractedly informed him as she reached forward to stroke one fingertip across the side of his erection. Watching it jump, she was pleased that he reacted to her touch. Emboldened, she wrapped her hand around his shaft.

Blake's hand closed around hers and lifted it from his body. "You do not have permission to touch Daddy. I think it's time that you learned what happens when you don't follow Daddy's directions or any rule." Blake sat on the edge of the bed and drew her toward him.

Samantha cooperated fully, believing that he would take her back to bed. She didn't expect for him to hook his fingers in the waistband of her leggings and underwear to pull them down to her knees. Trying to back away, Samantha almost tripped as the tight knit acted like handcuffs around her thighs. She reached out automatically to steady herself. Blake pinned her hands behind her back and quickly pulled Samantha over his knees before she could regain her balance.

"What are you doing?" she demanded, trying to press herself back up to standing. His knees widened to prevent her toes from touching the ground.

"You've earned your first consequence." Blake's hand caressed her exposed bottom before raising it to land smartly on her flesh.

Gasping at the sharp pain, Samantha's first thought was

that there was a negative side to his strength. Then she began struggling. "Stop! This isn't funny. I don't like this!" she protested as she tried to free herself.

"Little girls need to behave. If they don't, it's up to their Daddies to help them learn," Blake explained evenly as he continued to spank her full bottom.

"No!" she wailed. Stubbornly, Samantha continued to struggle. Tears began to tumble from her eyes to soak the carpet underneath her. Finally worn-out, Samantha slumped in exhaustion and pain over his lap. Immediately, Blake stopped spanking her. He collected her tenderly in his arms and rotated her body to sit on his lap.

Samantha hissed as her weight settled on her fiery hot bottom. She leaned against his broad chest, allowing him to comfort her as tears raced down her cheeks. His softly whispered words soothed her as Blake held her close, tenderly stroking her back. Samantha welcomed his loving attention.

Loving? Doubts flooded into Samantha's brain. She was the idiot. She'd let Darrell crap all over her for way too many years. Then what did she do? She hooked up with a hot guy next door who just happened to have the same kink that she'd read and lusted over for years. And now she thought he loved her?

Her sudden lunge off his lap freed Samantha from those supportive arms. Afraid that she would get tangled in the material, Samantha stepped out of her leggings and underwear. Racing to the back door, she ignored his shouted words of concern as she snatched the unicorn key ring from the rack and burst out the back door.

Locking her door behind her, Samantha began to cry in earnest. When the wood behind her back thumped under the weight of his urgent knocks, Samantha shouted, "Go away! I don't need another man to hurt me!"

"Samantha, you need to let me in so we can talk about

this. I know this was new for you, and you're upset. Don't run away and ruin what we have together," he urged.

"We don't have anything. Go away, Blake!"

"Sami, let me in, Little girl." His voice seemed filled with sadness and grief.

"Just go away!"

CHAPTER 7

Collapsing the last box, Samantha tossed it on the pile. She could hear Blake moving around next door. She'd avoided him since that horrible morning. Her schedule could be flexible, and she timed her trips to the dumpster and out to her car when she knew he was gone. Despite her best efforts, Samantha listened carefully to make sure he came home after each shift. She didn't want to worry about him, but she did.

Visiting dozens of times, he'd spoken to her through the wooden barrier. Blake had tried to call when she refused to open her door. He had finally resorted to leaving messages on her cell phone. His words were always the same—he missed her terribly and asked that she talked to him in person. It had amazed her that despite her lack of response, he hadn't stopped trying to connect with her. A guy playing a stupid game wouldn't keep trying when he realized she was onto him, would he?

Samantha's eyes fell on the crumpled piece of paper that she dug out of the trash. Held on her refrigerator with a smiley face magnet, Blake's block writing boldly stated the rules he required of his Little girl. *No, not his Little girl, but for me.* He'd clearly written the name Sami on each line.

What if Blake isn't playing a game? What if I totally screwed this up? Is it too late?

The trembling fingers, Samantha removed that list from the fridge and carried it to her design table. Opening her file, she pulled out a piece of pale pink parchment. The crisp paper felt cool under her fingertips. It reassured her she was doing the right thing. Grabbing a calligraphy pen, Samantha began to work.

As she finished, she heard Blake's car start out in the driveway. His shift must be starting. Standing up, she walked to the front windows and watched from behind the curtains as he left. She would give him ten minutes to make sure he didn't come back. Time clicked slowly past.

Taking three deep breaths to give herself courage, Samantha slid the key into the back door. She opened it slowly and slipped inside. Samantha paused to hang two rings on the key rack before turning to face into the kitchen. Armed with the now glittery pink paper, Samantha crept to his refrigerator and pinned her design to the bare front with the smiley face magnet that had mocked her. She stepped back to read the rules one more time.

#1 Follow Daddy's instructions.

#2 Daddy and Sami will always be honest with each other.

#3 Daddy and Sami will care for each other deeply.

#4 Sami will learn to trust her Daddy if he'll give her another chance.

That was all she could do. Reach out to Blake and see if he was still willing to be her Daddy. She'd understand if it was too late. The pain in his voice each time he talked to her had been palpable and real. By refusing to talk to him, Samantha knew she had wounded him deeply.

Turning to leave, Sami's thoughts jumped to the stuffed

tiger who she had rejected as well. She needed to explain to Grrr. Quickly, Samantha walked down the hallway. Peeking inside the nursery, she couldn't see the stuffie tucked into the crib. She felt as if she was invading when she stepped into the master bedroom.

Of all the rooms in the house, this room was stamped most with Blake's personality. A collection of police badges hung on one wall. Next to it, a shadow box filled with bath toys hinted at his desire to have a Little girl. Startled, she walked closer to see a new picture. Tears began to fall from her eyes.

"I messed this up so badly," she confessed out loud, staring at the image of herself asleep in the beautiful crib.

"A Little girl makes mistakes. It's up to her Daddy to help her learn," a deep gravelly voice sounded from behind her.

Samantha whirled around to see Blake standing behind her. She took two steps forward before she froze in place. Would he want her there? Samantha swallowed hard and forced herself to speak. "Can you ever forgive me?"

"The responsibility lies with me. I should have anticipated you would worry when things moved so quickly. I've missed you," he said warmly, taking a step toward her. He held out his hand. "Please, Sami. I need to hold you."

As if the cement holding her in place shattered, his words freed her from her worries and doubts. She flew across the floor into his arms. Burying her head against his broad chest, Sami clung to him. Tears flowed freely from her eyes to soak his uniform shirt. She could not get close enough to him.

"Shhh, Little girl. I have you now. I'll never let you go," he promised. Time passed as he held her protected in his arms. When the radio at his collar squawked, Blake simply triggered it to say, "Adams, out. LG."

"Understood."

"Do you need to go?" she asked, lifting her tearstained face.

Blake leaned forward to press a soft kiss on her cheeks before wiping the tears away. "No. I need to be here with you. My lieutenant will cover for me for a bit." He kissed her deeply before leaning down to scoop an arm underneath her knees. Carrying her over to the bed, Blake sat down with her cradled on his lap. "Can you tell me what scared you so badly? Was it the spanking?"

She nodded against his chest, unable to meet his gaze. Her fingers twisted in the fabric of his shirt as she tried to figure out how to tell him the truth. Finally, she blurted out, "I've read all those books. And a lot of them, a naughty Little girl get spanked. I didn't realize the impact it had."

"Was the pain too severe?" he asked in a voice filled with concern. She could tell immediately that he thought she'd fled because of him.

"The spanking hurt," she admitted, peeking up at him, "but that wasn't what made me panic. I got scared because I wanted this so bad. Everything happened so fast. I couldn't believe that this relationship was real."

When he remained silent, she continued. "When you spanked me, it forced me to admit to myself that I wanted it all. I wanted you to love me so much that you would correct me when I was wrong. I got scared because I was afraid it was impossible for both of us to feel that strongly in just a few days."

"I have friends who've been lucky enough to find their Little girl. They tell me they knew immediately when they saw her for the first time. She was theirs. It wasn't the same kind of relationship that others establish by dating over weeks, months, or years. I was happy for them but didn't understand. Then, I came home after a long shift to find you."

"I've been a problem since the first minute we met."

"That is not true," he corrected. "You are the solution. I

understood exactly what they had shared with me. I knew you were mine—my Little girl."

"A... Are you sure?"

Blake took her hand and pressed it to his heart. She could feel it thump strongly under her home. Her eyes jumped to search his face for deceit. She found only caring concern.

"My heart is yours, Sami. I love you. I saw the rule that you added. Do you think you can follow that?" he gently probed.

"Can you help me learn to trust you?" she whispered. "Can you give me another chance?"

"Will you promise me not to run again and to stay and talk?"

These had been the worst few days of her life. Even worse than when she'd discovered Darrell was having an affair. She cared more about Blake than she did about her former husband. That said a lot about her marriage. Slowly, Sami nodded. "I promise." She pressed her hand against his heart, regretting all the pain that she caused each of them.

"Then we figure this out." Blake leaned in to kiss her softly.

Sami threw her arms around his neck. She never wanted to let him go again. Blake's radio squawked again. She froze as he listened carefully to the message and reached to trigger the reply button, giving the message he was five minutes away. "Can we talk tonight?"

He nodded. "While I'm gone, I want you to remember that I love you very much. That's not a word I've ever thrown around. It means everything to me. Just as you do."

"Yes, Daddy. The last one thing before you leave?"

"What's that, Sami?"

"Can I play with Grrr while you're at work?" she asked with hope.

Blake turned to point at the tiger tucked into the covers on the large bed. "He was very upset when you left." Blake lifted Sami to her feet so she could reach the stuffie. When she turned with Grrr cuddled to her chest, Blake added, "You can play with him here or you can play with him in your area. He's been very lonely."

Blake stood to leave. Sami stopped him with one last question. "How did you know I was here?"

"When the silent alarm went off, I came myself instead of sending another car. I hadn't given up hope that you would come back to me, Little girl."

Sami dashed into his arms and pressed herself and Grrr tightly against Blake in a fierce hug. Linking her fingers with his, she tugged him down the hallway and to the open front door. "Go to work, Daddy. I'll be here." She stood with the tiger stuffie in her arms and waved goodbye as Blake returned to his patrol car. Sami was eager to explore the nursery and wanted to stay close.

CHAPTER 8

Sami looked at the clock one more time. She had no idea what time he normally got off work, but she knew it could vary depending on what was happening. At six o'clock, she heard a car door slam out front. Racing to the front of the house, Sami flung open the front door. At the sight of Blake walking up the driveway, she flew out of the house and threw herself into his arms.

"Wow! What a welcome! Did you miss me?"

"I missed you so much. Grrr and I have been playing, but we've been watching for you."

Blake linked his fingers with hers and squeezed her hand gently. "I've been waiting all day long to get home to you. Did you have fun playing in the nursery?" he asked her, holding open the door so she could walk inside.

"Did you know how many games there are inside the toy chest? Grrr won a lot of them. He let me win once in a while," she shared. "We're working on a puzzle on the kitchen table right now. Is that okay?"

"Making yourself at home here is perfectly fine in my book. Are you hungry? What is that amazing smell?" he asked as he stepped into the house.

"I had a big lasagna in my freezer. I ran over and got it to bake in your oven. It's ready now," she told him proudly.

"Come sit on the couch. Should I turn the oven off?" he asked.

Sami shook her head as she took a seat. "Everything's okay. About five minutes ago, I turned off the oven so the lasagna wouldn't overcook."

Blake sat down next to her. "Come sit on my lap, Little girl. I need to hold you in my arms. I also need five kisses."

"Five kisses?"

"One for each hour we were apart." Blake leaned forward and kissed her until they both forgot what number kiss they were counting. They were both breathing heavily by the time Blake raised his head. Sami laid her head on his broad shoulder with her hand in the center of his chest to feel his heartbeat. That regular thump meant something special to her now. It reminded her how much her Daddy loved her.

"There are many things that we need to learn as we build our lives together," Blake shared. "Being Little is different than your previous life. Your design business is very important to you, so you'll continue using your talents." Sami raised her head to nod eagerly.

"One of the tough things for Littles to learn is that although they're in an adult body, they're Little. That means no cleaning, no mowing, no…"

"No cooking?" Sami said, looking horrified. "I ruined everything already?"

"You didn't ruin anything. In just a minute, I'm going to pull out that the lasagna and we're both going to eat an enormous piece. But from now on, big chores are for Daddy. Sami chores will be to set the table or clean up all the games on the floor in the nursery," Blake said with a raised eyebrow.

"How did you know?" she asked, deflecting the blame by sneakily pointing a finger at Grrr. "You don't want me to have dinner ready when you come home from work? I'm here just hanging out at home?"

"You're not here just hanging out. You're doing important designs for your business or you're taking time to let your Little side have a little fun. Both of those things are more important than working alone in the kitchen. How about if we cook dinner together when I get home?" Blake suggested.

Samantha's mouth dropped open slightly as she digested his words. Blake thought however she chose to spend her time was valuable. "I should take time to be Little, too? Even when you're gone?"

"Being Little is not just an activity to play at—being Little is a life choice. You're not restricted to being Little only when I'm at home. You can be Little whenever you wish. It's not just limited to the time that we are together. You need to be true to yourself."

She considered his words for several long seconds. "I don't think I've ever done what I wanted to do just to make myself happy."

"Then it's time for a change, isn't it?" Blake asked with a gentle smile. "Now, I'm going to change my clothes and put on something comfortable. I'll invite my Little girl to come talk to me if she can behave very well and keep her hands to herself. If not, we'll never get to eat that wonderful-smelling lasagna."

Winking at her, Blake boosted her up onto her feet and stood to take her hand. In the bedroom, he insisted that she and Grrr sit in the middle of the big bed. Sami scrambled into place. She wasn't quite sure why she had to sit in the center of the mattress until Blake began to unbutton his shirt. The view of his toned body prompted her to shift to all fours.

"Daddy and Sami will play later. Sit back down, Little girl."

With a big exhale of exasperation, Sami settled back

down on her bottom as Blake dropped the shirt on to the floor. He turned to face the dresser as he unbuttoned his heavy weapons belt. Setting it gently with a clunk on the wood surface, Blake unbuttoned his pants and pushed them over his hips.

Sami stared as his muscular bottom and thighs clad in a pair of tight cotton boxer briefs came into view. Quietly, she moved her hands into the space created by her crossed legs. Unable to resist, she rubbed her thumb along the seam of her shorts. The subtle caress stoked the fire that had ignited inside her as he undressed. She could feel herself getting wet.

"Hands on your knees," Blake ordered.

His words drew her eyes from his body. As her gaze met his knowing eyes in the mirror, Sami felt her face heat. Quickly, she obeyed and wrapped her fingers around her knees. She made herself close her eyes when he leaned over to pull the pant legs over his feet. Ultimately unable to resist, Sami peeked through her eyelashes at the display. She tightened her grip on her knees. She wanted to be good for her Daddy.

When Blake turned around, Sami abandoned her narrowed vision. His body had responded to her eager appreciation. As she watched, the bulge grew to tent the cotton fabric barely containing him. Automatically, she shifted back to her hands and knees to crawl forward.

"Little girl," he growled at her in warning.

Sami threw herself back to sitting and stared at his crotch in fascination as his cock thickened and lengthened. Tearing her eyes from the display, Sami looked up at Blake's face. His expression caused a flood of arousal to soak her panties. Pure, raw desire was carved into his face. "Please, Daddy," she whispered.

With an abrupt movement, Blake peeled his briefs from his body and shoved them down his legs. His eyes focused on her, he stepped out of them and paused to allow her to scan his body for a few brief seconds. Prowling forward, he covered the space between them and dropped his palms to the comforter. "Come here, Little girl," he ordered.

This time when she rocked forward, Sami knew he would not order her back into position. He rose to wrap his arms around her and pulled her across the soft comforter. His mouth captured hers and invaded. Blake wrapped Sami in masculine strength. His aroused scent filled her nostrils, making her press even closer. Sami allowed her hands to roam over the expanse of his back and drift lower to cup his hard buttocks.

"Hold on," he directed in a voice harsh with desire. Without giving her any time to ask why, Blake lifted her from the comforter and turned to drop on his back with her crushed against his chest.

Off-balance by the sudden movement, Sami clung to his body before realizing that she now straddled his pelvis. When his hands urged her to sit up, Sami pressed against his chest to rise. Instantly she froze at the sensation of his shaft pressing against her wetness. She was wearing too many clothes. When Blake's hands pushed up her t-shirt, Sami ripped it over her head and threw it somewhere in the room. Her bra also was a quickly discarded annoyance.

His hands cupped her full breasts, kneading and caressing them. Sami held on to his shoulders as Blake curled forward to lick and suckle her taut nipples. She moaned loudly when he lightly bit one tight peak. His slightly rough hands abraded her sensitive flesh. Those light brushes with his thumb were driving her out of her mind.

Suddenly, she needed to be totally naked. Her shorts and underwear were an unwelcome barrier between their bodies. She rolled away from him and wiggled out of her garments before allowing his hands to move her back into position above him. Sami gyrated on top of him, her body slick over his rigid erection.

51

"No!" she protested as he lifted her hips to move her slightly away. Her breath escaped in a rush when his fingers slipped from her hips to caress the length of her thighs and stroked back to her core. There, Blake traced through her slick juices, dwelling on those places that brought gasps to her lips. She knew he was ensuring that she was ready for him.

Wishing to please him, she raised one hand to her lips. As Blake watched her, Sami licked her palm until it was wet. She wrapped her wet fingers around his thick erection and slid her grip from the tip to the root. When he groaned, she tried it again this time with a twist at the end. His hips rose from the bed to thrust against her hand.

After the third stroke down, Blake pulled her hand from his shaft. "Enough play, Little girl. Do you trust me enough to celebrate our return to each other?" he probed.

She could tell that he struggled to hold his desire at bay, to allow her more time if she needed it to be comfortable with their relationship. Sami nodded immediately. "Please, Daddy."

Immediately he reached a hand opened the drawer in the night table next to the bed. Finding a small packet, he quickly opened and sheathed himself in the condom. Sami rose to her knees, and he helped her move forward.

Watching his face as she helped him fit the broad head of his shaft at her drenched entrance, the sight of his eyes fixed on their joining bodies fueled her arousal. She could not doubt that it was her who he wanted. Eager to bring him pleasure, Sami pressed her hips forward to welcome his thick invasion. Her body yielded and stretched to allow him to glide in deeply.

Sami paused to allow them to feel their union. She wanted to remember this moment forever. All of this would never have happened if she hadn't let herself into his house. In her mind, Sami cursed the time that she had wasted.

"We start today." Blake's words interrupted her self-recrimination.

Her gaze jumped to his face. There written over the desire was worry. Even when they were intimately joined, Blake's concern was for her. Making a deliberate decision, Sami pushed the sadness from her mind and focused on the present. She repeated his words, "We start today."

Simultaneously, their bodies pulled away before repeatedly crashing back together. Caressing each other, Sami and Blake forged a new future for themselves. One based on passion and on trust, as each pleasured the other.

The lukewarm lasagna was perfect for a late-night dinner for two starving lovers.

CHAPTER 9

"**D**o you think Lettie forgot about our playdate?" Sami asked in a slightly trembling voice.

"Lettie will be here very soon. She is very eager to meet you," Blake reassured her with a smile.

"Will your boss think I'm too old?" The words burst from her mouth as she felt her face heat in embarrassment.

"No," Blake said without hesitation or uncertainty. "Lettie's Daddy will not judge you. He will be so glad to meet you. His Little girl has wanted to playmate for a very long time."

Ding dong! The doorbell rang loudly, making Sami jump in reaction.

She bounced slightly on her feet in excitement. "They're here, Daddy! Lettie came!" Sami celebrated. Grabbing Blake's hand, she dragged him to the doorway, only to signal him to wait as she smoothed her new dress back into place. When she nodded her head, Blake laughed and opened the door.

"Doug, I'm glad you're here, but I'm especially happy to meet you, Lettie," Blake said, greeting the guests at the door. "Please come in." He stood back and allowed the tall police officer to enter with Lettie. "This is Sami, my Little girl," he introduced her proudly.

Lettie wore overall shorts and a bright pink T-shirt. She clung to her Daddy's hand as if she was scared. Immediately her own nervousness evaporated, and Sami wanted to put her at ease. Sami stepped forward and smiled. "Hi, Lettie! I'm so glad you're here. Would you like to come see my nursery? I can show you all my toys and maybe we can play?"

"Can you teach me how to braid my hair like yours?" Lettie asked, taking a step forward.

"I can try? My Daddy did my hair today," Sami explained as she tugged on one braid dangling to her shoulder. She held out a hand to the young woman. "Come on! Let's go play beauty shop," she invited.

Placing her hand in Sami's, Lettie looked over her shoulder at the tall man behind her. "I'll be okay, Daddy. You don't have to worry about me now," she reassured him. The two Littles darted down the hall with giggles already drifting back to the two men.

Blake looked at his superior officer. The man was completely shaven bald. "Sorry, Doug. I'm not doing your hair," he remarked with a laugh.

"Somehow, I'll manage my disappointment. Got a beer for an un-braided Daddy?"

"You bet. There's even a game on TV. Come sit down. We'll go check on the girls in a little while, but I think they're going to be great friends."

Two Daddies exchanged a glance that said so much. Each understood the struggle the other had undertaken to find his Little. Now, their goals were to help each young woman be happy and healthy. The Daddies couldn't ask for more.

The End

PEPPER NORTH SERIES

DR. RICHARDS' LITTLES®

A beloved age play series that features Littles who find their forever Daddies and Mommies. Dr. Richards guides and supports their efforts to keep their Littles happy and healthy.

Zoey: Dr. Richards' Littles® 1
Amy: Dr. Richards' Littles® 2
Carrie: Dr. Richards' Littles® 3
Jake: Dr. Richards' Littles® 4
Angelina: Dr. Richards' Littles® 5
Brad: Dr. Richards' Littles® 6
Charlotte: Dr. Richards' Littles® 7
Sofia and Isabella: Dr. Richards' Littles® 8
Cecily: Dr. Richards' Littles® 9
Tony: Dr. Richards' Littles® 10
Abigail: Dr. Richards' Littles® 11
Madi: Dr. Richards' Littles® 12
Penelope: Dr. Richards' Littles® 13

SANCTUM

Pepper North introduces you to an age play community that is isolated from the surrounding world. Here Littles can be Little, and Daddies can care for their Littles and keep them protected from the outside world.

Sharing Shelby: A SANCTUM Novel
Looking After Lindy: A SANCTUM Novel
Protecting Priscilla: A SANCTUM Novel
One Sweet Treat: A SANCTUM Novel
Picking Poppy: A SANCTUM Novel
Rescuing Rita: A SANCTUM Novel
Needing Nicky: A SANCTUM Novel
Adoring Ali & Ace: A SANCTUM Novel

SOLDIER DADDIES

What private mission are these elite soldiers undertaking? They're all searching for their perfect Little girl.

The Medic's Littles Girl
Tex's Little Girl
Jax's Little Girl

THE KEEPERS

This series from Pepper North is a twist on contemporary age play romances. Here are the stories of humans cared for by specially selected Keepers of an alien race. These are science fiction novels that age play readers will love!

The Keepers: Payi

The Keepers: Pien
The Keepers: Naja
The Keepers Collection

THE MAGIC OF TWELVE

The Magic of Twelve features the stories of twelve women transported on their 22nd birthday to a new life as the droblin (cherished Little one) of a Sorcerer of Bairn. These magic wielders have waited a long time to take complete care of their droblin's needs. They will protect their precious one to their last drop of magic from a growing menace. Each novel is a complete story.

The Magic of Twelve: Violet
The Magic of Twelve: Marigold
The Magic of Twelve: Hazel
The Magic of Twelve: Sienna
The Magic of Twelve: Pearl
The Magic of Twelve: Violet, Marigold, Hazel
The Magic of Twelve: Primrose
The Magic of Twelve: Sky
The Magic of Twelve: Amber
The Magic of Twelve: Indigo
The Magic of Twelve: Rose
The Magic of Twelve: Scarlet
The Magic of Twelve Collection: Volume 1 - Violet - Marigold – Hazel
The Magic of Twelve Collection: Volume 2 - Sienna - Pearl – Primrose
The Magic of Twelve Collection: Volume 3 - Sky - Amber – Indigo
The Magic of Twelve Collection: Volume 4 - Rose - Jade – Scarlet

Other Titles

The Digestive Health Center: Susan's Story
Electrostatic Bonds
Perfectly Suited
3rd Anniversary Collection
Marked Brides

ABOUT THE AUTHOR

Pepper North is a hybrid author whose contemporary, paranormal, dark, and erotic romances have won the hearts of many loyal readers. After publishing her first book, Zoey: Dr. Richards' Littles 1 on Amazon in July 2017, she now has over sixty books and collections available on Amazon in four series.

Pepper is exhilarated to be a USA Today Bestselling Author. She credits her success to her amazing fans, the support of the writing community, and her dedication to writing.

Connect with me on your favorite platform!

AFTERWORD

If you've enjoyed this story, it will make my day if you could leave an honest review on Amazon. Reviews help other people find my books and help me continue creating more Little adventures. My thanks in advance. I always love to hear from my readers what they enjoy and dislike when reading an alternate love story featuring age-play. Contact me on
my Pepper North FaceBook page,
on my website at www.4peppernorth.club
email at 4peppernorth@gmail.com

Want to read more stories featuring Zoey and all the Littles? Subscribe to my newsletter!
Every other issue will include a short story as well as other fun features! She promises not to overwhelm your mailbox and you can unsubscribe at any time.
As a special bonus, Pepper will send you a free collection of three short stories to get you started on all the Littles' fun activities!

Here's the link:
http://BookHip.com/FJBPQV

Follow me on BookBub for notifications of my new releases!

Printed in Great Britain
by Amazon